Princess Penella

By Daniella Revitt

Tellwell Talent
www.tellwell.ca

ISBN
978-1-998190-80-5 (Hardcover)
978-1-998190-30-0 (Paperback)
978-1-779412-12-6 (eBook)

For my girls, Mariah, Cayleigh and Sophia.

Princess Penella's no regular gal, with her twinkling eyes...

...and
butterfly pal

She's strong
and she's bold,

she's respectful
and fair...

...but please don't
be fooled by
her casual air.

She's buff,
she's courageous,

fearless and fun...

...beautifully
sensible,

a most
confident one!

She sparkles
and glimmers,

like a
radiant
light.

She's loving,

and thoughtful...

...and fights for what's right.

...her name is Penella
and this is what she's about.

This girl is rock-solid, she's one of a kind...

She's sincerely forgiving,

honest and sweet...

...there's no match for this girl, no matter how tough the feat!

She's resilient and rugged
in the most delicate way...

...she's thankful for life and each miraculous new day!

She respects who she is
and won't sell herself out...

KINDNESS

the quality of being friendly, generous, and considerate.

I am brave

·I AM·
STRONG

I am
HAPPY

I can make a difference

I believe in me

·I am·
HEALTHY

·I am·
CONFIDENT

I am kind

I am loved

I am
Smart

Manufactured by Amazon.ca
Acheson, AB

11598043R00031